CARL THE CAT

By Joshua Horn

Joshua Horn

Hello, everyone.
I'm Carl the Cat.
I'm not very
skinny, and I'm
not very fat.

I get very curious when
I look out the door. I
love my cat life, but I
sometimes want more.

Joshua Horn

I play with my cat toys, and my scratching post. But there's a few other things that I love the most.

My parents work hard,
so that I'm not poor. So
I help them out, and sit
in this drawer.

Joshua Horn

The office is boring, with not many thrills. The secret is out now. I pay the bills.

To say I love chores,
well, that isn't true. But
I get my paws wet when
there's dishes to do.

Joshua Horn

My mom does the laundry,
and keeps the clothes clean.
I can't find the washer! Is
this what they mean?

The laundry is done! And
it fills me with pride. Now
pick me up mama! Let's
go for a ride.

Joshua Horn

The last thing to do is to empty the trash. Look guys, I did it! It's time for a splash!

At last it is time for a dip in the pool. And when it's this hot out, it's nice to be cool.

After the swimming, it's time
for some shade. For a big
fluffy cat, I sure got it made.

Look at me now! I'm up in
a tree. I do love my house,
but I like to roam free.

Joshua Horn

From up in a tree, to high on a roof. Mom thinks she can catch me, but I'm such a goof.

My body is nimble, and not very dense. This makes it so easy to jump over this fence.

Uh-oh, they've caught
me! I've run out of luck.
I just hope that this bag
doesn't zip up.

I escaped again! I'm as slick as a fox. But mom says playtime is over, so I'll lie in this box.

Joshua Horn

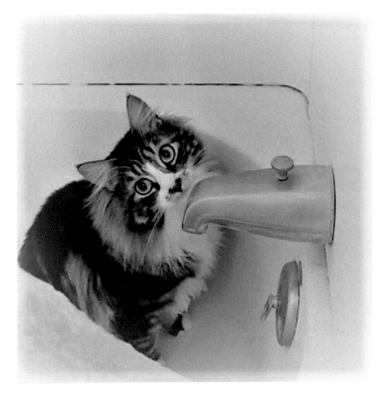

This cat is thirsty! It's time for a drink. Hey guys, what's wrong? This isn't the sink?

What an adventure! It's time for a nap! This bed sure is comfy, but I wanted a lap.

Joshua Horn

Now that my nap's over, it's back in the pool! Nah, I'm just kidding. I'll work from this stool.

Sometimes I like to read a good book. What do you think? Is this a good look?

Joshua Horn

The seasons can change, but I'm still on the go. It might be too cold to play in this snow.

My mom loves the snow,
so she puts up this tree.
But she didn't have to
do all this for me.

Joshua Horn

As I look out the window,
the sun goes away. There
was plenty of fun for
this cat today.

Nighttime has come and I'm cozy and fed. Goodnight, everyone. It's time for bed.

Joshua Horn

Goodnight, Carl!

The End

Made in the USA
Columbia, SC
15 November 2020

24610970R10015